D0579140

A NOTE TO PARENTS

Disney's First Readers Level 3 books were developed for children who have mastered many basic reading skills and are on the road to becoming competent and confident readers.

Disney's First Readers Level 3 books have more fully developed plots, introduce harder words, and use more complex sentence and paragraph structures than Level 2 books.

Reading is the single most important way a young person learns to enjoy reading. Give your child opportunities to read many different types of literature. Make books, magazines, and writing materials available to your child. Books that are of special interest to your child will motivate more reading and provide more enjoyment. Here are some additional tips to help you spend quality reading time with your child:

★ Promote thinking skills. Ask if your child liked the story or not and why. This is one of the best ways to learn if your child understood what he or she has read.

★ Continue to read aloud. No matter how old the child may be, or how proficient a reader, hearing a delightful story read aloud is still exciting and a very important part of becoming a more fluent reader.

★ Read together on a regular basis, and encourage your child to read to you often. Be a good teacher by being a good listener and audience!

★ Praise all reading efforts, no matter how small.

★ Try out the After-Reading Fun activities at the end of each book to enhance the skills your child has already learned.

Remember that early-reading experiences that you share with your child can help him or her to become a confident and successful reader later on!

— Patricia Koppman
Past President
International Reading Association

Painted by John Raymond, Adam Devaney,
Ken Becker, Brent Ford, and Todd Ford

First published by Random House, Inc., New York, New York.
This edition published by Scholastic Inc.,
90 Old Sherman Turnpike, Danbury, Connecticut 06816
by arrangement with Disney Licensed Publishing.

SCHOLASTIC and associated logos are trademarks of Scholastic Inc.

ISBN 0-7172-6657-5

Printed in the U.S.A.

DISNEY'S
ATLANTIS
THE LOST EMPIRE

KIDA
AND THE
CRYSTAL

by K.A. Alistir
Illustrated by the Disney Storybook Artists
at Global Art Development, Denise Shimabukuro,
and Samantha Clarke

Disney's First Readers — Level 3
A Story from Disney's *Atlantis: The Lost Empire*

⭐⭐⭐

SCHOLASTIC INC.
New York Toronto London Auckland Sydney
Mexico City New Delhi Hong Kong Buenos Aires

Long ago, a huge tidal wave headed straight for a city called Atlantis.

The people of Atlantis ran for shelter. But it was hopeless. The wave was about to swallow their entire island in one giant gulp!

The royal family raced for the palace. "This can't be happening," the king of Atlantis told himself. Atlantis was a powerful city. How could it ever be in danger?

The queen reached for her daughter.
"Come quickly, Kida!" she cried. Then a
bright light lit up the sky. The light was
coming from a Crystal floating above the
city. A beam of blue light shone on the
queen. It pulled her up into the Crystal.

"Mama!" little Kida cried. But the queen
had disappeared into the Crystal.

Suddenly more beams of blue light shot down from the Crystal. They surrounded Atlantis like a protective bubble. When the tidal wave hit, it crashed against the bubble. The city and its people were saved!

But then the island of Atlantis sank deep down into the blue ocean. It became a lost city, hidden away from the rest of the world.

Many, many years passed. Princess Kida grew into a strong young woman. She was curious, too. She wanted to find out why Atlantis had sunk into the ocean. She could also see that the city was now becoming weak. But mostly, she was worried about her weakening father.

One day, Kida visited her father in his throne room.

"Father, tell me again about the day my mother was taken away," she said.

The king did not like to talk about the past. "We cannot change our history," he told his daughter.

Upset, Kida left the throne room. She would go hunting instead.

Kida called to her warrior friends, "Let's prepare for the hunt!" She pulled her hunting mask over her head. Then the group set off.

Kida and her friends explored a maze of caves, looking for cave beasts. But soon the hunting party came across something much more interesting. It was a group of explorers from the surface world! Kida and her warriors decided to follow them.

After a while, one of the explorers became separated from the others. He was hurt!

Kida went to take a closer look. The young man wore strange clothes. His shoulder was bleeding. Kida took off her crystal necklace and placed it on the wound. In a flash, the man was healed.

Then more surface people arrived. They were friends of the young man.

"Welcome to the city of Atlantis," Kida told them. "Come, you must speak with my father."

The king was not happy to see visitors. He wanted them to leave.

"But these people may be able to help us," the princess said. The king shook his head. He insisted that the visitors leave Atlantis the next day.

Kida was disappointed. She wanted answers to her questions.

She found one of the explorers waiting outside the throne room. He was the man she had healed. His name was Milo.

"I have some questions for you," Kida said, grabbing his arm. "And you are not leaving this city until they are answered."

Milo agreed. He was just as curious about Atlantis as the princess was!

The princess led Milo to a cave. There, she told him about the Great Flood.

"My father said the gods were jealous of Atlantis. So they sank the city into the ocean." She told him about the bright light and how her mother had disappeared.

"You were there?" Milo cried. "That would make you more than eight thousand years old!"

"Yes," Kida replied calmly. "How did you find this place?"

Milo showed the princess an ancient leather book—*The Shepherd's Journal*. It was full of information about Atlantis.

Kida stared at the worn journal. Milo was surprised to learn that she could not read.

"Since the Great Flood, no one has
been able to read," Kida explained sadly.
"Our history was lost."

Suddenly she had an idea. She led Milo
farther into the cave.

Under a thick cloth stood a fish-shaped vehicle. "This is a Ketak," explained Kida.

"Wow! It looks like something you drive," said Milo.

"Yes," said Kida. "But I can't make it work."

Milo read the instructions carved into the top of the Ketak to Kida. Following them, she placed her crystal into a slot. The vehicle started and rose into the air!

"With this thing, I can see the whole city in no time!" Milo shouted.

Then Milo placed his hand on the Ketak. *Zap!* It took off by itself.

Bang! The Ketak flew around in circles, bouncing against the walls.

Milo and Kida jumped for cover. The Ketak stopped with a crash.

So Kida showed Milo the city—on foot.

They walked to an outdoor market.
"Are you hungry?" asked Kida.
"I certainly am," said Milo.

Kida went to a stall at the market. She bought two long, gooey tentacles, each wrapped around a stick.

"I certainly am . . . not hungry anymore," Milo added quickly.

Kida bit off a tentacle. "Tastes good," she said, offering one to Milo.

Milo took a small bite. "Not bad. But it could use some ketchup."

Just as Milo finished eating, a little
girl ran up to Kida.

"Kida! Kida! Are you coming to my
birthday party?" the little girl asked.

"Of course, Tali," said Kida. "A girl
doesn't reach fifteen hundred every day."

Milo went to the party with Kida.

"Um . . . Milo," said Kida at one point. "You're using an Atlantean hairbrush to eat your cake."

The cake tasted even better when Milo ate it with an Atlantean fork.

Milo and Kida left the party and climbed to the top of the hill overlooking the city. Milo gazed down at Atlantis.

"The most my team hoped to find was some crumbling buildings," he told Kida. "Instead, we found a whole city full of people!"

But the princess just shook her head sadly. Her beautiful city was slowly falling apart. Every year it was harder to find food. Every year her people forgot more of their history.

Kida brought Milo to a pool of water.
"I have brought you to this place to ask
for your help," she told Milo. "Follow me."

They dived into the water. Soon they were swimming past ruins of ancient buildings. Bright murals and Atlantean writing covered the walls.

"This is amazing!" Milo said when they came up for air. "The history of Atlantis is painted on these walls!" He held up Kida's glowing crystal necklace to read the ancient writing.

Kida could barely speak. Milo could tell her the whole story. At last she would find out what had happened to her city!

"Does the writing say anything about the light I saw?" Kida asked Milo.

They took deep breaths and swam back under the water.

In one drawing, Milo saw a large Crystal falling from the sky. In another drawing, people were wearing pieces of the Crystal around their necks.

Milo and Kida swam up for air.

"The light that you saw," Milo explained, "is the Heart of Atlantis. It is a power source. It keeps everyone and everything in Atlantis alive."

Kida remembered the last time she had seen the huge Crystal. Her mother had floated up into its blue light. The Crystal had taken the queen. As soon as she had disappeared, Atlantis had been saved from the tidal wave. The queen had given her life for the sake of the city!

Kida hugged Milo. "Thank you for your help," she said.

Milo blushed.

The princess smiled. Not only had she found out the truth about Atlantis, but she had also made a wonderful new friend!

As Milo swam back to the surface, Kida took another long look at the pictures on the wall. The pictures showed the history of her city—and told the story of her family.

"Thank you, Mother," she thought, "for all you have done for us."

Just then the crystal around Kida's neck began to glow. Kida knew it was a message. "Be brave," the crystal seemed to say. "Be strong."

And Kida was. With Milo's help, she was ready to unlock all the secrets of Atlantis.

AFTER-READING FUN

Enhance the reading experience with follow-up questions to help your child develop reading comprehension and increase his/her awareness of words.

Approach this with a sense of play. Make a game of having your child answer the questions. You do not need to ask all the questions at one time. Let these questions be fun discussions rather than a test. If your child doesn't have instant recall, encourage him/her to look back into the book to "research" the answers. You'll be modeling what good readers do and, at the same time, forging a sharing bond with your child.

KIDA
AND THE
CRYSTAL

1. What saved Atlantis from the tidal wave?

2. Who did the giant Crystal take?

3. How did Milo find Atlantis?

4. Besides books, name three other things you read.

5. What did Milo and Kida find under the water?

6. Find 10 descriptive words.